Wishes really do come true

Lucky Stars

The Perfect
Pony Wish

Phoebe Bright

Illustrated by Karen Donnelly

MACMILLAN CHILDREN'S BOOKS

Special thanks to Valerie Wilding

First published 2012 by Macmillan Children's Books
a division of Macmillan Publishers Limited
20 New Wharf Road, London N1 9RR
Basingstoke and Oxford
Associated companies throughout the world
www.panmacmillan.com

ISBN 978-1-4472-0234-9

1 3 5 7 9 8 6 4 2

A CIP catalogue record for this book is available from
the British Library.

Printed and bound by CPI Group (UK) Ltd, Croydon CR0 4YY

For Tom and Zara Scott, with love

Contents

Hello, friend!

I'm Stella Starkeeper and I want to tell you a secret. Have you ever gazed up at the stars and thought how magical they looked? Well, you're right. Stars really do have magic!

Their precious glittering light allows me to fly down from the sky, all the way to Earth. You see, I'm always on the lookout for boys and girls who are especially kind and helpful. I train them to become Lucky Stars – people who can make wishes come true!

So the next time you're under the twinkling night sky, look out for me. I'll be floating among the stars somewhere. Do give me a wave!

Love from
Stella x

1
Stella Starkeeper

Cassie laughed as a star-patterned pillowcase blew off the washing line into her face.

'Wow! That wind's strong!' she said.

The two charms on her silver bracelet jangled as she pegged the pillowcase back on the line. She glanced at the charms – a tiny bird and a tiny crescent moon – and smiled. Their magic helped her to make special wishes come true.

I hope I meet someone with a wish today, she thought.

'When we offered to help your mum hang up the washing, I didn't expect to chase it round the garden!' called her friend, Alex.

Cassie's fair hair was blowing over her eyes. She pushed it away so she could see Alex collecting three socks that had blown into an apple tree. She laughed.

They started on the second washing basket.

'How many towels have you got?' asked Alex. 'I've already pegged out eight. That's about a third of what's here, so I calculate that . . .' He mumbled, frowning in concentration.

Cassie giggled. Alex loved maths and science, and was always trying to work things out.

'Remember, this is a B & B,' she said. 'That means ten times more towels than in an ordinary house.'

Starwatcher Towers was far from

ordinary. One part of it was the B & B and the other part was an observatory where Cassie's dad worked, watching the stars and planets in the night sky. Even Cassie's bedroom had a glass ceiling so she could lie in bed watching the stars!

'You shouldn't really be helping,' said Cassie. 'B & B guests don't normally hang out their own towels.'

Alex shrugged. 'Mum and Dad are meeting someone today, so it's good to have something to do. Anyway,' he said shyly, 'it's nice to help friends, isn't it?'

Cassie grinned. 'You bet!'

She hadn't been too sure about Alex when he'd first arrived at Starwatcher Towers. Then she realized he only seemed unfriendly because he was shy, and they soon became good pals.

The catflap clattered, and out popped Alex's fluffy white puppy, Comet, followed by Cassie's dear old cat, Twinkle. Just as Cassie and Alex had become friends,

so had their pets.
Cassie stroked
Twinkle's
black fur.
'Meowwww,'
he yowled.

'Yupp!' barked Comet.

Cassie brushed her untidy hair out of her eyes. 'You two should stay indoors,' she told the animals. 'You might get blown away!'

'Only if the wind's strong enough,' said

Alex, stroking his chin. 'I'll get
my anemometer,' he said, 'then I can
measure the wind speed.' He ran inside
and the wind banged the door shut behind
him.

Cassie threw another towel over the
line. As she pegged it down, she noticed
a bright light shining through the clouds
that scudded across the sky. *A star?* Cassie
thought. *In the morning?*

Dad had taught Cassie lots about the
stars. She knew that you couldn't usually
see them in the daytime because the sun is
too bright. As she watched carefully, the
star seemed to be swirling, whirling down
towards her!

Cassie remembered the last time she

saw a star behaving like that. Could it be . . . ?

With a *whoosh* and a *whizz* and a *fizz-fizz-fizz*, the star was beside her in a flurry of silver sparkles.

It grew into a column of dazzling light. Then the light softened, and it changed into . . .

'Stella Starkeeper!' cried Cassie. 'You're back.'

A beautiful young woman stood before her in a short silver dress and a shiny silver jacket with star-shaped buttons. She wore glittery leggings and silver boots, and in her hand was a wand, tipped with a shining star. Her rippling hair fluttered in the wind, and on her head was a crown woven from strands of glistening silver.

Stella's velvety-blue eyes twinkled as they gazed into Cassie's brown ones. 'Hello, Cassie,' she said. 'I came to see how you're getting on with your new charm.'

The bracelet was Stella's gift to Cassie on her seventh birthday, a few days ago. She touched Cassie's bracelet with her wand, and a sprinkling of sparkles drifted to the grass.

'Never forget,' Stella said. 'You must listen for someone to make a special wish, then use the powers of the magic charms to

help make the wish come true. Then you'll earn a new magic charm.'

'When I earn seven charms, I'll be a real Lucky Star, just like you,' said Cassie.

Stella Starkeeper smiled. 'And you'll be able to grant wishes whenever you like!'

The Perfect Pony Wish

Cassie glanced at her bracelet. 'The bird charm gives me the power to fly,' she said, 'but what does my crescent-moon charm do? I don't feel any different. It does do something, doesn't it?' she asked.

Stella's eyes sparkled and her crown glittered as she leaned forward. 'Listen carefully, Cassie,' she whispered. 'Listen, and you'll hear something you never expected to hear.'

With a wave of her wand, Stella faded into a silvery mist. But a sudden gust blew her silver crown off!

'Wait!' cried Cassie.

It was too late.

Stella had disappeared.

Cassie chased after the crown as it tumbled over and over on the grass. She reached out to catch it, but it bounced against a tree and soared over the fence and down the hill.

She watched in despair as it disappeared from sight. *Oh no!* She'd never find it now!

'Got it!' yelled Alex.

Cassie turned. He was holding one of his science contraptions. 'Oh,' she said. 'Is that your amin . . . namen . . . ?'

Alex grinned. 'An-em-o-meter,' he said.

'Anen . . .' Cassie began. Then she laughed. 'Your wind-speed gadget!'

She watched Alex set it on the garden table. It had a stand with four arms, each

with a cup
shape at the
end. The wind
blew the cups
round and
round.

As Alex
pottered with
his measuring, Cassie remembered what
Stella had said. She wandered over to lean
against the plum tree's knobbly trunk. Then
she closed her eyes, thought about her
crescent-moon charm and listened.

A voice came from behind.

'This wind's blowing my coat all over
the place,' it said. 'I must look a complete
scruff.'

Lucky Stars

It was a weird, yowly sort of voice. Cassie was sure she'd heard it before.

She opened her eyes. It definitely wasn't Alex, but no one else was around. Only

Comet, who was playing on the other side of the garden. And Twinkle, who was sitting beside Cassie, staring up at her with his wide amber eyes.

Cassie gasped. '*Twinkle?*'

2
Sunbeam and Sita

Cassie knelt down. Sparkles danced around her cat, making his whiskers twitch.

Twinkle looked straight back. 'I'm scruffy, aren't I?' he asked.

'N-no,' said Cassie.

The cat's eyes widened. 'You're talking to me,' he said.

'And you're talking to me!' said Cassie. 'Alex! Here!'

Alex came over and knelt down.

'Twinkle,' said Cassie, 'speak to Alex.'

'Hello,' said the cat. 'Cassie can understand me. Can you?'

'Did you hear him speak?' asked Cassie.

'Of course I did,' replied Alex. 'Meow, meow, meow. What were you expecting?' He went back to his anemometer.

Twinkle looked at Cassie. 'I'll tell Comet you talked to me. He'll be so jealous!' He prowled over to Comet. The cat mewed and the puppy barked. Sparkles swirled around both of them.

'Why is Twinkle staring at Comet's tail?' Alex wondered aloud. 'And why is Comet barking like that?'

'They're talking!' answered Cassie. 'Comet's saying, "Watch my tail, Twinkle. The wind's whipping it backwards and forwards without me wagging it!"'

Alex spun round. 'You can understand him?'

Cassie nodded, realizing with a thrill that this was the power of the crescent moon. How exciting! *I've always wanted to talk to*

Twinkle, she thought. *Now I can!*

'But it can't be possible,' Alex said.

Twinkle was curling himself round Cassie's legs, saying, 'I love being able to talk to you. It's grrrreat!'

Alex grinned. 'He's purring now. I suppose you can understand that?'

'Yes,' said Cassie. 'He's happy he can talk to me.'

Alex stroked his chin. 'You're probably watching their behaviour, and that helps you understand them,' he said.

How can I prove I know what they're saying? Cassie wondered. Then she had an idea.

'Comet,' she said. 'Tell me something you and Alex do when you're by yourselves.'

'Every morning,' said Comet, 'I jump on his bed and lick his ear, then he hides under the covers.'

Cassie smiled and turned to Alex. 'Comet wakes you up by licking your ear.'

Alex gaped at her. 'You *can* understand animals!' He scratched his head. 'But surely there's a scientific explanation.'

Cassie threw a ball for Comet. He barked, 'Whoopee!' and chased after it.

'You scientists are supposed to be good at observing things,' said Cassie. 'Don't you recognize magic when it's right in front of you?'

Comet brought the ball back. 'Again! Again!' he panted.

Cassie threw it. 'Alex,' she said, 'I told

you about Stella Starkeeper, and my bracelet's power.' She jangled the charms. 'Don't you remember flying in the sky with me, looking at the clouds?'

He nodded. 'Ye-es,' he said, 'but I still think there's a scientific—' He stopped, because Cassie was gazing past him. 'You're not listening,' he said.

'Sorry,' said Cassie. 'I just noticed some people visiting Bert.' She pointed down the hill that led into the town of Astral-on-Sea. A big green car towing a horse box was pulling into Bert's stables. His donkeys lived there when they weren't giving children rides on the beach.

'Let's go and see,' Cassie said. She wondered if she could understand horses too.

They ran down the hill, feeling the wind
pushing them along. The stables stood at
the bottom, close to the sandy beach.

'The wind's helping us!' Alex cried.

'It's a proper gale,' Cassie shrieked.

The Perfect Pony Wish

'That's what my anemometer measurements showed,' Alex puffed as they rounded the corner by the stables.

Cassie paused at Bert's gate. A girl about her own age was leading a pretty dappled pony out of the horse box. The donkeys watched curiously. Even Coco, the new timid donkey, peered over his stable door. Cassie was glad he was getting braver.

The girl's mum chatted to Bert as she unpacked the pony's equipment. She saw Cassie and Alex, and waved. 'Hello!'

Cassie waved back. 'Do you need any help?' she called above the wind's howl.

'We're fine, thanks,' the woman said with a smile as she sorted through a box of brushes, combs, bottles and cloths.

The girl looked across at them. 'Hi,' she said. 'Come and meet my pony.'

Cassie went over and stroked the pony's soft, silver-grey nose.

'He's cute,' she said. 'What's his name?'

'Sunbeam,' said the girl. 'And I'm Sita Shah.'

As Cassie and Alex introduced themselves, Sita's mum came over with a handful of pony nuts.

'Our darling Sunbeam is competing in the Astral-on-Sea Pony Championship this afternoon,' she said. 'We're staying with Mrs Cafferty at Starwatcher Towers. Do you know it?'

Cassie laughed. 'I live there,' she said. 'I'm Cassie Cafferty.'

'And I'm staying there,' said Alex. 'It's at the top of the hill. See?' He pointed.

'Gosh!' said Mrs Shah. 'It must be even windier up there.'

'I measured the wind speed,' Alex said

proudly. 'It's officially a gale.' He helped Mrs Shah close up the horse box.

'We'll show you the way to Starwatcher Towers,' said Cassie.

'Thanks,' said Mrs Shah, 'but Sita must exercise Sunbeam first. He needs to stretch his legs.'

The pony whinnied softly, and nuzzled Cassie's neck. She giggled. 'He's gorgeous,' she said. 'I bet he'll do well in the competition.'

Sita sighed. 'I doubt it,' she said, and laid her face against the pony's cheek.

'Why?' asked Cassie.

'Sunbeam doesn't like jumping,' said
Sita, 'but he's got to try.' She turned to
Cassie and whispered, 'You see, Mum used
to ride in competitions, but she can't now,
because her back's bad. Sunbeam was born
at our stables, and she adores him. If we do
well, she'd be so proud and happy.'

Sita stroked the pony's nose. 'Oh,
Sunbeam,' she said, 'I wish we could win
the competition.'

Cassie smiled. *Aha!* she thought. *I've
found the person I must help!*

She watched Sita lead Sunbeam to a
bucket of fresh water. The pony drank
thirstily. It would be wonderful to make
Sita's wish come true – and Cassie would

earn her next magical charm.

'I have to teach Sunbeam to jump,'
Cassie murmured to herself. 'But how?'

3
Runaway!

Cassie patted Sunbeam's firm, warm neck while Sita gently slipped the bridle over his head. Then Sita saddled the pony. She showed Alex how to fasten the girth straps underneath Sunbeam's tummy, and check that the saddle was neither too loose nor too tight.

'Just right,' she said. 'Pretty good for a first time, Alex!'

Cassie smiled at her friend. He grinned back happily.

A sudden gust of wind whipped Bert's
hat off and flung it through the open
gate. He stumbled back against a row of
empty feed buckets and sent them
clattering across the yard. The donkeys
brayed in fright. 'Errrgh-hee-errrgh-heee-
errrgh!'

At the same time, one of the stable doors
banged shut.

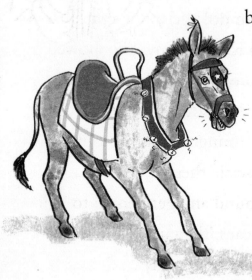

Sunbeam whirled
round and
threw his head
back in fright.
Before anyone
could stop him,
the terrified
pony bolted

out of the gate and on to the beach. Within
seconds he was just a spot in the distance.

'Sunbeam!' Sita screamed.
She ran to the gate. 'Mum!'
she called. 'We have to go
after him.'

'Wait,' Mrs Shah said.
'Let me think! Oh, I
don't know what to do!
We've never been to
Astral-on-Sea before. We wouldn't know
where to look. Perhaps Bert . . .'

Bert was busy calming the jittery
donkeys. 'Let me settle these down and
then I'll phone around and get people to
look out for Sunbeam,' he said. 'I should
have shut that gate more tightly . . .'

'Don't worry, Mrs Shah!' said Cassie. 'Alex and I will find Sunbeam. You and Sita drive up to Starwatcher Towers. You get a good view from up on the cliff, so maybe you'll spot him.'

She and Alex tore out on to the empty, windswept sands. 'We'll find him!' Cassie shouted over her shoulder.

She knew exactly what to do. She looked down at the tiny bird charm on her bracelet. A tingle ran up her arm and through her whole body, and silvery sparkles danced all around her.

Cassie grabbed Alex's hand. 'Hold on!' she called as they rose into the air. She felt as light and floaty as cotton wool. This was the magic of the silver bird charm! Away

38

they flew along the beach, sticking close to
the cliff edge to avoid being spotted.

'Whooooa!' cried Alex.

'You're OK,' said Cassie. 'You've flown with me before, remember?'

Alex held tightly to her hand. 'How could I forget? This is amazing. I can feel air currents moving in different directions.'

Cassie smiled. 'Forget science, for once. Just enjoy the magic.'

Alex laughed. 'I'll try!'

A butterfly with purple wings flitted beside them. It looped the loop, as if it was enjoying the blustery wind, then fluttered away.

A moment later, Cassie spotted something moving in a lane that led away from the beach towards a wooded area.

'Is that Sunbeam, Alex? Down there,

40

at the edge of the trees?'

'Yes!' said Alex. 'Let's go a bit lower.'

Cassie tugged on Alex's hand, guiding them back to the ground. With a flurry of whirling leaves and silver sparkles, they landed in a small clearing in the woods.

Alex brushed himself off. 'The wind's dropped,' he said. 'The gale must have blown itself out at last. Here comes the sun.'

'Never mind the weather,' said Cassie. 'Where's that runaway pony?'

Sunbeam was nowhere in sight.

4
Snorter Knows

'Sunbeam! Sunbeam!' Cassie and Alex
called. But the pony didn't show himself.

Then Cassie saw something light-
coloured at the far edge of the wood.

'Look!' she cried, pointing. 'There's
Sunbeam!'

They raced through the trees and came
out into a lush grassy field, dotted with
grazing sheep and a sprinkling of golden
buttercups.

'It must have been a sheep you saw,' said Alex. 'Sunbeam's not here. I'll keep checking among the trees.'

The sheep! Of course!

Cassie thought hard about her crescent-moon charm. Instantly, the bracelet glowed and silver sparkles streamed from it. They flitted around Cassie's head, flashing in the sunlight.

'Excuse me!' she called.

Sparkles danced towards a big woolly sheep.

'Are you talking to me?' asked the sheep.

Cassie nodded. 'Has a pretty dappled pony come past?'

'Bah!' said the sheep. 'He might be pretty, but he's not well mannered. He

nearly sent my little Baabaa flying.' She
nodded towards a lamb, who was prancing
giddily among the buttercups.

'Which way did the pony go?' asked
Cassie.

'Towards the duck pond,' said the sheep.

'Thanks!' Cassie was halfway across
the field before she realized Alex hadn't
followed her. 'Come on, Alex!' she called
out.

'Cassie, we haven't finished searching the
wood,' said Alex, stepping out of the trees.

'But the sheep said . . .' Cassie stopped
and laughed. 'Silly me. You couldn't
understand her, could you?'

'Understand who?' asked Alex.

'That nice sheep.' Cassie jangled her
bracelet. 'I've been talking to her. Come
on, let's go to the duck pond. I'll explain
on the way.'

But there was no sign of Sunbeam there
either. Cassie crouched down, showering
a tiny yellow duckling with silver sparkles.

'Have you seen a dappled pony?'

The duckling's eyes opened wide. 'Yes.
It drank some of my pond
and it nearly drank me up
too!'

'Poor you,' said
Cassie. 'Which way
did he go?'

'To the pigsty,' said
the duckling. 'He'd
better not upset Snorter.'

Cassie thanked the duckling and hurried
to the pigsty, trailing clouds of silver
sparkles. Alex ran after her.

'What now?' said a cross voice from
behind the sty gate.

It was a large pink pig, who snapped at

the sparkles that swirled around his nose.

'You must be Snorter,' said Cassie.

'If you've come after that greedy pony,
you're most welcome,' said the pig.

'Please get him out of our farmyard.'

'He's such a sweet pony,' said Cassie. 'He won't do any harm.'

Snorter grunted angrily. 'Won't do any harm? Won't do any *harm*?' He stamped a muddy trotter. 'That pony's eaten my lunch!'

Cassie noticed an empty bucket by the pigsty gate. 'Oh dear.'

'Oh dear? Is that all you can say?' the pig snorted. 'That pony's probably started on my supper now. Find a wheelbarrow full of apples, and I'll bet you find your pony.'

'Alex, look for a wheelbarrow,' Cassie cried.

He checked all around the pigsty wall.

49

'Not here,' he said. 'I'll look behind that barn.' A moment later, he yelled, 'Cassie, come quickly!'

She ran behind the barn and there, munching happily on the apples in the wheelbarrow, was the runaway pony.

'Sunbeam!' Cassie threw her arms round his neck, sending silver sparkles whirling around them both.

'Uh-oh, I suppose I'm in trouble,' neighed the pony.

Cassie stroked him gently. 'You're not in trouble, Sunbeam.'

The pony looked up at her in surprise. 'Can you understand me? How do you know what I said?'

'It's a long story,' said Cassie, 'and we must get back to Sita.'

Sunbeam tossed his head.

'What's wrong?' asked Cassie. 'You love Sita, don't you?'

'Of course.' The pony nodded. 'I'll go back, I promise. Later.'

Cassie looked into his huge, dark eyes. Was it her imagination, or was Sunbeam looking sad? 'Why did you run away?'

'The bangs and clatters frightened me,' he said. 'So did the donkeys and their braying.'

'But, Sunbeam,' said Cassie, 'it was just the wind blowing everything about, and the poor donkeys were frightened too. But the wind's died down now, so there's nothing to be scared of any more.'

'Yes, there is.' Sunbeam pulled away. 'There's . . . there's . . . the competition.'

'Of course,' said Cassie. 'Sita told me that you don't like jumping.'

'I hate it!' Sunbeam neighed. 'Jumping *really* scares me.'

Cassie stroked his neck softly. *Oh no*, she thought. *Poor Sunbeam!*

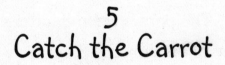

5
Catch the Carrot

Cassie looked at Alex. 'We must help Sunbeam get over his fear of jumping,' she whispered. 'I really want to make Sita's wish come true.'

Before Alex could reply, a cheery voice called out, 'Hello, young Cassie.'

A smiling, round-faced man came down the path from the farmhouse, carrying a large china bowl.

'Farmer Greg!' Cassie said. 'Please don't

be cross. The pony's eaten Snorter's lunch *and* some of his supper.'

'Don't worry. Plenty more where that came from,' said the farmer with a chuckle. 'Bert phoned and told me to watch out for a runaway.' He handed the bowl to Cassie.

It was full of carrots. 'I thought these might help catch the pony, but I see you've found him already. You help yourselves.'

'Thanks,' said Cassie and Alex, each taking one.

56

'I saw you talking to the pony, Cassie,' said Farmer Greg. 'It looked like you were hoping he'd reply!'

'Oh, I was calming Sunbeam down,' Cassie said, feeling sure that wasn't a fib. She couldn't explain what she was really doing. Farmer Greg would never believe her!

The farmer laughed. 'Well, keep at it,' he said. 'With a bit of practice, he might be able to answer you! Ha ha!'

A bit of practice? That gave Cassie an idea. 'We'll take Sunbeam back to Bert's stables, but can we use your paddock for a while first, please?'

'Course you can! If you need riding hats, there's some in the barn,' said Farmer Greg.

He put the bowl of carrots on a low wall.
'I'm off to check the sheep. Back in a bit.'

Cassie found two buckets and took them
into the paddock next to the yard. She
put them upside down, a little way apart.
'Would you fetch me that broom, please,
Alex?' she called.

As soon as Cassie laid the broom over the
buckets, Alex realized what she was doing.
'You're making little jumps,' he said.

'That's right,' said Cassie. Then she
whispered, 'I know what will tempt that
greedy little pony to jump!'

She filled her pockets with carrots, then
concentrated hard on her crescent-moon
charm. Instantly, her arm tingled.

'What are you up to?' asked Alex.

'Watch.'
Cassie walked
to the pony
in a drift of
silver sparkles.
'Sunbeam,
we're going to
play Catch the
Carrot. Would
you like to play too?'

'I don't know how,' said Sunbeam sadly.

'It's easy,' said Cassie. 'Just copy Alex.'
She held out a fat carrot and cried, 'Come
on, Alex, catch the carrot!' Then she ran.

Alex chased after her. As they circled
round towards Sunbeam, Cassie slowed
down, and Alex grabbed the carrot.

'I win!' he said, and took a big crunchy bite. 'Yummy!'

Sunbeam trotted to Cassie. 'Can I play now?' he asked.

'OK.' She waved a carrot in front of his nose. 'Go!'

Cassie ran off and the pony trotted after her. As she reached the first jump, she thought about her bird charm. Her legs tingled, silver sparkles swirled around her and she took off. *Wheee!* She floated over the broom.

But Sunbeam stopped. He wouldn't jump.

Cassie floated back and forth over the broom a couple of times. 'This is fun!' she cried, waving the carrot. 'Yummy, scrummy!'

This time Sunbeam trotted towards the jump – and leaped over!

Hooray! thought Cassie. *And again . . .*

Sunbeam followed her over the next jump.

Cassie decided he deserved a reward, so she let him catch the carrot. It was gone in a flash!

'Let's play again!' said Sunbeam, neighing with excitement.

'OK.' Cassie floated over the jumps, while the pony leaped after her. Next time he caught a carrot, he said, 'I didn't know jumping could be fun!'

While Sunbeam crunched the carrot up, Alex whispered, 'Don't feed him any more, or he'll be too full to jump in the competition.'

The Perfect Pony Wish

'You're right,' said Cassie. 'Let's take him back to the stables. Sita will be so worried and she'll need time to get Sunbeam ready.' She paused. 'There's just one problem. I don't think I can manage to fly with you *and* Sunbeam. And even if I could we don't want to get spotted.'

'But it will take ages to walk back,' said Alex. He glanced at his watch. 'The competition starts in one hour.'

Cassie stroked the pony's silky mane. 'So how are we going to get back in time?'

Sunbeam's ears twitched. 'I've got an idea!'

6
Sunbeam Takes Charge

'I'm strong,' Sunbeam said. 'I'll give you both a ride. If I trot all the way, we'll be there in no time.'

'You clever pony!' Cassie cried.

'What did he say?' Alex looked puzzled.

'We can both ride Sunbeam back to the stables,' said Cassie. 'But I've never ridden a pony before.'

'Nor me,' said Alex, suddenly looking worried.

Cassie spoke to Sunbeam again. 'We don't know what to do,' said Cassie. 'It's a bit scary.'

'You helped me to be brave,' said Sunbeam. 'Now I'll help you. All you need are riding hats.'

'Farmer Greg said we could borrow some,' said Cassie. She ran into the barn and found two hard hats. They put them on.

'Fasten it under your chin,' said Sunbeam.

Cassie did so.

'And you, Alex,' said the pony. But Alex didn't move.

Cassie giggled. 'Sorry, Sunbeam, I keep forgetting that I'm the only one who can understand you.' She showed Alex how to fasten his hat.

Sunbeam trotted to a low wall. 'Stand on that, then climb on my back. You first, Cassie, then Alex behind you. Hang on tight.'

Once they'd mounted, Cassie felt very high up!

'Take the reins,' said Sunbeam, 'but don't pull. I'll do all the work. Off we go!'

As he walked forward, Cassie felt Alex hold on round her waist. She gripped the front of the saddle.

'Relax,' said Sunbeam. 'You'll enjoy it. Wish I had a carrot,' he muttered.

Cassie giggled. 'I heard that!'

'I'm going to trot now,' said Sunbeam. 'It'll feel odd, but you won't fall, I promise.'

'We're going to go faster, Alex,' Cassie warned. 'Hang on!'

His arms tightened round her middle as they jogged along. 'I'm going to bounce right off!' cried Alex.

'You won't,' Cassie gasped.

They soon became used to the jogging motion, moving up and down to Sunbeam's rhythm.

'Look!' said Alex, suddenly. 'Bert's cap – there, on that wall.'

Cassie asked Sunbeam to go to the stone

wall. The pony had to hop over a little
ditch to get there.

'Whooa!' cried Alex.

'Great jump!' said Cassie.

Alex leaned over and grabbed the cap.
'The wind brought it all this way!' he said
as they jogged on.

Just before they reached the stables,
Cassie spotted a gleam in the hedge. 'The
crown!' she cried. 'Stop, Sunbeam!'

'A silver crown stuck in a hedge?' said
Alex. 'Where on earth did that come from?'

Cassie grinned. 'The crown is Stella
Starkeeper's. It blew off when she came to
see me.' She leaned over to pick it up, but
it was too low down.

'I'll get it,' said Alex. He slid off

Sunbeam's back and passed the crown to Cassie. 'You can carry it home!'

The crown sparkled in the sunlight and a tingle ran up Cassie's arm. She took off her riding hat and placed the crown on her head.

'It fits!' she cried. *That's magic too*, she thought.

Mrs Shah's car was just pulling into the stables as they arrived. Sita leaped out.

'Sunbeam!' she cried.

'There's my Sita,' said the pony. 'Hold tight!' He went even faster and, in a flash, they reached the gate. Sunbeam nuzzled Sita's neck, and she hugged him happily.

The Perfect Pony Wish

'Thank you so much for bringing him back,' she said, looking up at Cassie and Alex. 'However did you find him?'

'I just, well . . .' Cassie shrugged and grinned at Alex. 'I just asked around!'

7
The Final Round

Cassie and Alex were thrilled when Mrs Shah invited them to the Pony Championship. They raced uphill to Starwatcher Towers, where Cassie stowed Stella's crown safely in her bedside cupboard.

Ten minutes later, Mr and Mrs Cafferty waved goodbye as Cassie and Alex drove off beside Sita in the big green car, with Sunbeam in the horse box behind.

Sita was quiet. Cassie touched her arm.
'Are you OK?'

'I'm nervous,' Sita said. 'I'm afraid
Sunbeam will refuse to jump. I really want
to win a rosette.'

Mrs Shah smiled. 'Winning is a bonus.
It's having a go that's important, darling.'

'I know,' Sita said in a small voice. 'But I want to win.' She turned to Cassie and whispered, 'For Mum.'

Cassie crossed her fingers.

At the showground, everyone helped groom Sunbeam. While Sita brushed flecks

of mud from his body, Cassie brushed his glossy mane. Then Sita showed her how to use a smooth damp cloth to remove dust from the pony's coat and give it an extra shine. Alex helped Mrs Shah put oil on Sunbeam's hoofs. How they gleamed!

As Cassie brushed Sunbeam's forelock, he leaned his head against her.

'He likes you,' said Sita.

'I like him too,' said Cassie. 'I'm beginning to understand ponies.'

Alex spluttered with laughter, but no one noticed because there was an announcement from the speaker system: *'The competition starts in five minutes.'*

'I'll be right back!' Sita cried, grabbing a

bag from the car. She disappeared into the horse box.

Soon she came out wearing a neat black jacket and hat, cream jodhpurs and shiny boots.

Cassie gasped. 'You look fantastic!'

'I don't know who looks smarter, you or Sunbeam,' her mum said, smiling.

Cassie could see Mrs Shah was proud of Sita, and thought, *I hope she'll be as proud of Sunbeam.*

Sita slipped her foot into one of the stirrups that hung from Sunbeam's

saddle. She swung into the saddle and rode away.

'Good luck, Sita!' Cassie and Alex cried. 'Good luck, Sunbeam!'

They headed for the roped-off arena where the show-jumping course was ready with colourful jumps – a stack of hay bales,

a wooden fence and a log lying across sturdy posts. Some spectators had folding chairs or rugs to sit on while they watched and, on the far side, the judges sat at a long table. Outside the arena, ponies and riders waited nervously for their turn.

When the announcer said, 'Next is Sita Shah on Sunbeam,' Cassie held her breath.

Sunbeam entered the ring, the starting bell rang and they were off! The first jump was quite low, and he sailed over it.

Cassie heard Mrs Shah gasp in surprise as the brave little pony cleared jump after jump. 'Only two to go,' she said.

Sunbeam jumped again.

'Just one more,' said Alex.

'Come on, Sunbeam,' Cassie murmured.

But the pony's hind leg caught a striped

pole and sent it
clattering to the
ground. A groan
went up from the
crowd.

'Just one jump
down for Sita and Sunbeam,' said the
announcer. 'Maybe we'll see you in the
second round.'

Mrs Shah explained that if no one got
a perfect round, then those who had only
knocked down one fence would jump
another round to see who was the winner.

At the end of the first round, the judge
announced that there would be a jump-off
between Sunbeam and two other ponies.

Sita rode over. 'Wasn't Sunbeam

wonderful?' she said. 'He's so brave. It almost felt like he was enjoying himself.'

'I think he was,' said Cassie.

Sita frowned and said, 'I hope knocking that fence down doesn't put him off in the next round.'

Cassie wondered the same thing. 'Shall I take Sunbeam for a drink of water?' she suggested.

'Good idea,' said Sita. 'But don't let

him have too much, or he won't feel like
jumping.'

Cassie led the pony away, thinking hard
about her crescent-moon charm. Silver
sparkles swirled around Sunbeam's head.

'You were brilliant!' she told him.

'Thanks. I liked
knowing you were
watching,' said
Sunbeam. 'It made
me feel braver.'

Cassie patted
his neck as
he drank.
'You'll
enjoy
the next

84

round,' she said, 'now you know you *can* do it.'

'Cassie! It's my turn!' called Sita. 'Quick!'

With a whispered, 'Go for it!' Cassie led the pony to Sita. She climbed up into the saddle and the pony trotted over to the starting place.

'The other two ponies have had their turn,' said Mrs Shah. Her eyes shone. 'They both knocked down a fence, so, if Sunbeam clears all his jumps, he and Sita will win!'

They leaned on the gate to watch. Cassie was so nervous for Sita she could barely breathe. Had her Lucky Star magic been enough?

Sunbeam's tail flew as he jumped the first four fences perfectly. And the next! Soon there

were only two to go. Then just one – the fence he'd knocked down in the first round.

'I can't look,' said Cassie. But she did.

Sunbeam leaped into the air and – oh no! His hoof caught the pole. It rattled and shook – but it didn't fall. He was over!

'He's done it!' yelled Alex.

Everyone cheered!

'The winner, with the only clear round,' said the announcer, 'is Sita Shah, on the magnificent Sunbeam!'

More cheers!

When the red rosette was clipped on to Sunbeam's bridle, Sita grinned at her mum. Cassie thought that neither of them could look any happier.

Her arm tingled. She looked down to see her bracelet glowing brightly. As the glow faded, it revealed a shiny new charm – a delicate butterfly with shimmering wings.

It's like the butterfly that flew next to us, Cassie thought, thrilled. *I wonder what power it will give me?*

At bedtime, Cassie glanced around her room. It was circular, and there were stars everywhere – on her duvet, her rug and even on her purple pyjamas. Her moon-shaped bedside lamp shone softly on the starry wallpaper.

The Perfect Pony Wish

I've always loved stars, she thought, *and now I've met Stella Starkeeper they're even more important to me.*

She snuggled into bed, with Twinkle curled up beside her, and gazed up at the night sky through the open panel in

her glass ceiling. Thousands of stars were sprinkled across the sky. But one glowed brighter than the rest.

She sat up. 'Twinkle, look!'

The old cat stirred. 'I'd rather snooze, thanks,' he murmured.

Cassie slipped out of bed and took Stella's crown from her bedside cupboard. She thought about her bird charm and floated up through the open panel, high into the dark sky.

She flew towards the brilliant star. As she drew near, the light was dazzling, but then it softened and changed into a silver-haired woman in a shimmering dress.

'Look what I found,' cried Cassie, holding out the crown.

90

The Perfect Pony Wish

Stella Starkeeper smiled. 'I thought I'd lost it,' she said. 'You not only helped Sita today, but you helped Sunbeam too, and now you've helped me. You're going to make a wonderful Lucky Star!'

'I hope so,' said Cassie.

'You've earned your third charm,' Stella said, touching Cassie's bracelet. 'You only need four more. Now go home and sleep. Starry dreams!'

Cassie drifted sleepily down towards Starwatcher Towers, wondering about the butterfly charm. What new adventure would it bring?

She couldn't wait to find out!

Cassie's Things to Make and Do!

Join in the Lucky Stars fun!

The Perfect Pony Wish
Animal Care

Can you match these animals with what they eat and where they spend time?

Use one colour for each animal and draw a line matching the food and home.

Wishes really do come true
Lucky Stars

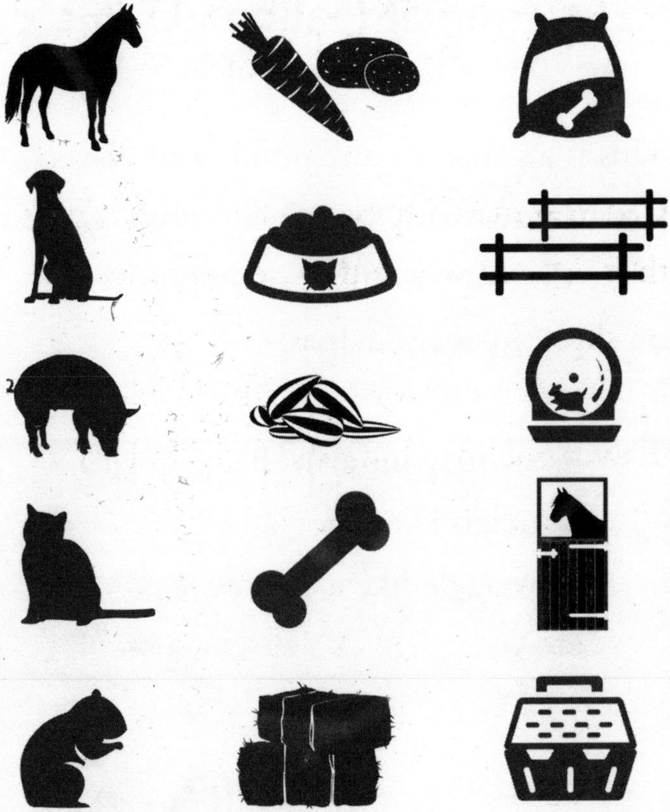

The Animal Balloon Game

This is a game for any number of players. Count how many people are playing and write the same number of animal actions on slips of paper, such as:

- ☆ swing your arms like a gorilla
- ☆ neigh like a horse
- ☆ wriggle like a worm,

etc.

Now put each slip of paper into a balloon before you blow it up.

Blow up one balloon for each player.

Give each player a balloon and ask them all to sit on their balloon until it pops.

Each player must do the action they find inside, and the rest of the players must guess what animal they are.

Answers

Don't look unless
you're really stuck!

The Perfect Pony Wish Animal Care

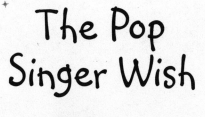

Lucky Stars

Wishes really do come true

The Pop Singer Wish

To read an exciting chapter,
please turn the page . . .

1
Songs on the Sand

'Magic, magic moments, these are magic moments . . .' Cassie sang.

Her black and white cat, Twinkle, joined in. 'Yowl, yowl, meow, yowl . . .'

The huge dome of the observatory at Starwatcher Towers rang with the sounds of their voices. Cassie was singing along to a CD of 'Magic Moments', the latest hit by Jacey Day. She was Cassie's favourite pop star, and that afternoon Cassie and her friend Kate were going to watch Jacey perform. She was the opening act in the Songs on the Sand music festival, right here in Astral-on-Sea!

All week, Cassie and Kate had been practising a special dance routine to 'Magic Moments'. As she twirled, Cassie imagined that Kate was also dancing around the Fairy-cake Bakery where she lived with her mum.

Cassie turned up the music. 'Let's dance, Twinkle,' she giggled.

Twinkle blinked his eyes. Cassie scooped him up from the old leather chair in which he was sitting and whirled across the room, being careful not to bump into any of the shiny telescopes. Her dad was an astronomer, and most nights he could be

The Pop Singer Wish

found up here, watching the stars.

'There's a friend I'd love to meet,
Spinning world beneath his feet,
He's got pebbles in his hands,
Running across the glistening sands . . .'

Along with Jacey's sweet, clear voice, the backing singers added a catchy harmony to the song. Their voices blended together perfectly.

When the song ended, Cassie noticed a tingling feeling in her arm. She put Twinkle back on the chair and looked at the charm bracelet round her wrist. Her new butterfly charm seemed to flutter its colourful wings.

'I wonder what magical power this charm has,' Cassie said. 'And who I'll help next.'

Cassie used her magical charms to help make people's wishes come true. With each person that she helped, she received another charm for her bracelet. So far Cassie had three. The bird charm gave her the power to fly and the crescent moon allowed her to talk to animals. But the magic of the butterfly was still a mystery.

'Meow!' Twinkle's ears twitched. He seemed to be trying to tell her something.

Cassie concentrated hard on her crescent-moon charm, so she could understand him. 'What is it, Twinkle?' she asked.

'I can hear music,' he said. His ears twitched again. 'It's coming from outside.'

Cassie listened. Yes, there *was* music, a beautiful tinkling sound. Where was it coming from? She gazed up into the brilliant blue sky and saw a star shining

brightly at her. Cassie knew how unusual
it was to see a star in daylight, but she also
knew this was no ordinary star.

The star zoomed down, straight through
the open skylight of the dome, filling the
observatory with silvery music. Then, with a
whizz and a *fizz* and a *zip-zip-zip*, it landed
next to Cassie.

'Meow!' Twinkle shot under the chair.

Cassie watched with delight as the star
grew into a column of dazzling light, which
slowly changed into . . .

'Stella Starkeeper!' Cassie flung her arms
round her friend. 'It's *so* good to see you!'

Stella was helping Cassie to become a
Lucky Star. Today she looked as lovely as
ever, her silver dress and leggings glittering

above her shiny boots and her long silver hair rippling over her shoulders.

'I see you've earned your third charm,' Stella said. 'Well done. You'll soon have all seven charms and become a Lucky Star. Then you'll be able to grant wishes whenever you like!'

'I can't wait,' said Cassie. She turned the little butterfly in her fingers and looked at its glittery wings. 'But what does my new charm do?'

Twinkle crept out from under the chair and tried to bat the little charm with his paw.

Stella laughed and tickled Twinkle under the chin, making him purr loudly. 'I'll give you a clue,' she said, her velvety-blue eyes

shining. 'You have all the time in the
world . . .'

The beautiful music filled the dome
again. With a wave, Stella disappeared in a
shower of glittering sparkles.

Cassie looked at Twinkle. '*All the time in
the world*. I wonder what Stella could mean?'

Wishes really do come true

Lucky Stars

Explore the magical world of Lucky Stars!

For fun things to make and do – as well
as games and quizzes – go to:

www.luckystarsbooks.co.uk

Wishes really do come true
Lucky Stars

Cassie is training to become a Lucky Star –
someone who can make wishes come true!
Follow her on more exciting adventures as
she meets new friends in need of help.

The Best Friend Wish

The Perfect Pony Wish

The Pop Singer Wish

The Birthday Wish

The Film Star Wish

The Ballerina Wish

Find a new magical charm FREE
with every book – collect them all
to become a Lucky Star!

www.luckystarsbooks.co.uk